THE FIRST RUNG

A WILKINSON'S DETECTIVE AGENCY SHORT STORY

ALEXANDRIA BLAELOCK

Also by Alexandria Blaelock

SHORT STORY COLLECTIONS
The Haunting of Hayward Hall
Lovelorn, Lovestruck and Love at First Sight
Common or Garden Variety Heroes
Case Files of the Wilkinson Detective Agency
Unavoidable Fates
Christmas Travesties
Five Faces of Felicia Clarke

FICTION
That Love Nonsense
Taipan vs Brown

MS BLAELOCK'S BOOKS
Stress Free Dinner Parties
Signature Wardrobe Planning
Holistic Personal Finance
Minimally Viable Housekeeping
Planning a Life Worth Living

A SELECTION OF AVAILABLE SHORT STORIES
Alma'that thas Grace
Fate in Your Hands
Kiss of Death
Lady of the Looking Glass
Life in the Security Directorate
Morning Star, Evening Star, Superstar
Payton's Run
Secret Singer
Shining Star
Ship in a Bottle
Simone Says Hands in the Air
The Day the Schedule Broke

THE FIRST RUNG

A WILKSINSON'S DETECTIVE AGENCY SHORT STORY

ALEXANDRIA BLAELOCK

BlueMere Books
MELBOURNE, AUSTRALIA

Publisher's Note: This is a work of fiction. Names, characters, places, and incidents are a product of the author's imagination. Locations and public names are sometimes used for atmospheric purposes. Any resemblance to actual people, living or dead, or to businesses, companies, events, institutions, or locations is completely coincidental.

Copyright © 2021 Alexandria Blaelock.

All rights reserved. No part of this publication may be reproduced, distributed or transmitted in any form or by any means, including photocopying, recording, or other electronic or mechanical methods, without the prior written permission of the publisher, except in the case of brief quotations embodied in critical reviews and certain other non-commercial uses permitted by copyright law.

For permission requests, please contact enquiries@bluemerebooks.com.

Ordering Information:
Discounts are available on quantity purchases. For details, contact orders@bluemerebooks.com.

The First Rung/Alexandria Blaelock
paperback ISBN: 978-1-922744-47-0
digital ISBN: 978-1-922744-48-7
AI generated audio ISBN: 978-1-922744-49-4

THE FIRST RUNG

Dot Sayers sat at her desk, huffed on the plastic card that was her new class A Private Security licence, and buffed it with her sleeve. She was now a fully licensed private investigator!

Not criminal investigations, her Investigative Services course had insisted, only civil investigations. Like insurance fraud, missing persons, or general security and background checks.

She sat up, looking over her tiny cubicle's grey soundproof walls like a meerkat, for someone to share her excitement with. But all she saw was the tops of heads, bent deep over their work.

The Collins Street office of the Wilkinson National Detective Agency (est. 1889), was crowded with seemingly hundreds of other tiny grey cubicles resting on a floor of grey carpet.

If you weren't ready for it when you walked in, the whole floor blended into a kind of uniform greyness, and with no differentiation of features; nothing to distinguish any one cubicle from the mass of greyness.

Like walking into the middle of a cool, dark storm cloud, without the wetness.

Though storm clouds didn't usually smell like someone's leftover curry.

The sound of busy workers conducting phone interviews was a low-level hum around her, reminding her of the sleepy drone of a beehive on a warm summer day.

And in a way, that's what they were.

Hundreds of tiny drones, undertaking desk checks and verifications on an industrial scale. Like cold callers, except with relevant qualifications and some self-respect.

Nonetheless, Dot smiled and slotted the card in the top row of her computer keyboard, leaning against the function keys and patting it lightly into place. She was excited to have finally made it.

She pulled the stack of background checks towards her, tried to set the phone headset more comfortably on her head, and prepared to make her first call.

It might be grunt work for others, but for her, it was the first step on the long, glorious ladder to the big time.

THE FIRST RUNG

Dot was named after grandmother Spencer, or Dotty as she was known, who was named after Dorothy L. Sayers.

For most of her childhood, she'd resented the old-fashioned name. When the jokes and taunts found her in school, she'd been prepared to be proud of her connection with the "original" Dorothy Sayers, but when she'd quizzed her parents, they'd confessed their ignorance.

Which somehow made it even worse.

She'd intended to change it as soon as she was old enough. But Dotty doted on her, and after she'd died, Dot came round to the name. Hoping to live up to both Dotty's and the "original's" example.

In fact, she adopted the circle as her signature icon and had hundreds of necklaces, earrings and hair accessories to dress up her otherwise plain, block, deep coloured clothing.

She dialled the first number, explained she was doing a background check for an employer, that she had the candidate's permission. Receiving their permission, she started working her way through the questionnaire, noting the answers on the form in permanent ink.

At the end of the day, she gathered up her files and reported in to her boss/mentor/supervising investigator Steve.

"Come," he said when she knocked on his door.

He was an older man, somewhere between middle-aged and ancient. His fierce green gaze was amplified by his horn-rimmed spectacles, and his eyebrow clenching frown made him look a bit like what she imagined an old-fashioned boy's school headmaster might look like.

His office was almost exactly like her cubicle, but with a larger chair, a window view and a longer desk.

And no neighbours.

She shut the door behind her and sat on the edge of one of the chairs facing him.

"So, how was your first day?" he asked.

"Fine..." She coughed a little to find her voice, "fine thank you, no problems."

"Good. And how did you get on?" he asked.

"Well," she said, putting the completed files on his desk. "I've done about a hundred files now," she said, knowing perfectly well she hadn't done anywhere near half that amount, "and they're all fine and straightforward except this one." She tapped the file on top of the pile labelled John Anderson.

"What makes you say that?" he asked, leaning forward to pick it up, and flip through it."

"I don't know," she shrugged, "the answers from each of the businesses were almost the same. It all seemed a bit down pat, a bit too positive. Like they'd memorised their parts and were reciting them back to me."

"Well, it all looks fine to me."

Dot slumped a very little as he leaned forward to look at her.

Then she tried again, "his last job was a few months ago, so it's possible they've forgotten what he was like. Or that he's really bad at his job, and his referees were glad to get rid of him. Or that... Oh, I don't know.

Steve relaxed back into his chair, looking at her, tapping the file against his lip as he considered what to do.

"Look, I don't see an issue," he said, "but you're the one who makes the call about whether to investigate further. I think it's a waste of time, but I'm going to give this back to you to do some more digging. Then you'll learn when to trust your gut and when not to."

He offered her the file and she stood up to receive it.

"Thanks Steve, I won't let you down."

He held the one file a moment longer, "it's not a priority, so don't fall behind in your regular work," he said before he let it go.

Dot was so excited to take it back she almost curtsied.

She took the files back to the record store, noting the return of the Anderson file to her the next day. Then she cleared her desk, making sure to strictly adhere to the policy, by locking all her pens and papers in the drawer.

She glanced around, and seeing no one, did a little fist punch in the air. She'd survived her first day on the job, had a file of her own to investigate further, and was on her way to becoming a top-notch private investigator.

The next day she was so excited to get to work and make a start, she woke before her alarm went off, left her apartment well before she needed to, and got off the tram a few stops early because it was taking too long.

She strode happily down the footpath; almost skipping, but too purposefully to be considered so frivolously.

And because she didn't anticipate a break until lunchtime, she picked up a latte and a small hedgehog slice, assuring the barista *everything* was fine and she hoped he was too.

All that and still in the office a little before she was due, though she had to wait a little while at the records office to receive the day's files. And then took a little more time to find her desk again.

She set aside the files, took a sip of her coffee and looked at the Anderson file again. She couldn't pin her nebulous feeling of suspicion down to any one thing. It was more the overall vibe.

The fingerprints were not in the file, so she couldn't check those, but she could request a Federal Police and credit check.

Both would require a payment she wasn't authorised to make, and take around a week, but they were something further to consider.

The candidate had listed three previous employers, they looked to be small or maybe small-to-medium businesses, though her reference checks had not included anyone from a senior position, so she grabbed a pad of file notes and a pen, and looked them up on the internet.

At first glance, the first website seemed legitimate, with the Australian Business Number, addresses, phone numbers, and details of the partners. But when she looked through some of the pages, they didn't make any sense in the context of the front page. A bit like random grab bags of information that would do for a quick glance.

She jotted down the details and her thoughts, then moved on to the next site.

The second website included the same basic information but was just a landing page inviting you to fill in the contact form. There was so little information it seemed more legitimate than the first, but still, she couldn't quiet that nagging voice in her head.

When she looked at the site again, she realised the phone number was different by one digit from that listed on the reference she'd called the previous day.

Before she could give herself too long to think about it, she put her headset on and dialled the number.

It rang several times.

She was slightly surprised an answering machine hadn't kicked in - a legitimate business that wanted to make money would have answered or queued an automatic system by now.

Dot was about to hang up when someone answered the phone.

"Hello?" an old, thin voice answered.

"Oh, hello! My name's Dot Sayers, I called yesterday to do a reference check?"

There was a long silence at the other end of the phone.

"Hello? I'm calling about John Anderson?"

The silence continued?

"Are you there?"

"No.

"No.

"No. There's no one here by that name."

"I'm so sorry to bother you then. Goodbye."

And she hung up.

And took a deep breath.

It was entirely possible for the website to contain an error.

But.

She wrote the information on her notes along with the result of the second call

The third website had ABN, but no addresses or phone numbers, only a contact form. When she accidentally clicked on the background image, she was directed to a template page still containing the Lorum ipsem text.

It was possible the businesses were not up-to-date with the current online sales and marketing practises, but that all three sites did not at least look professional seemed suspicious.

And one admin manager position was pretty much like the next, aside from the levels of confidential information you might expect to have access to at the client's company.

She did a quick, free Securities Commission search for each business and noted the owner names they were listed under weren't suspicious, aside from being Smiths, Jones, and Lee, which were some of the most common names in Australia.

Dot drummed her fingers on her desk, wondering what to do next, not willing to give up so soon.

And then she smiled and looked up the business addresses and checked the street view.

Admittedly the view was probably out of date, but she noted none of the business on street view were the same as the business names she was investigating. The first one was a house, the second a warehouse, and the third a small accountancy firm.

None of them looked to be on the scale of size that would require a manager for several admin staff, though one admin person might be called the admin manager for the sake of making a tiny business seem a bigger concern.

Getting more detailed business information seemed the next step, but again required a payment she was not authorised to make.

Then again, was that going too far when she was assessing John Anderson for a position with her client?

Though, it could mean Anderson had fabricated the references for the purpose of fraudulently gaining a position at the company.

Potentially, Anderson had backers who'd set up, or at least bought shelf companies.

THE FIRST RUNG

Not that a company with no previous history was suspicious, but overall, she was coming up with too many red flags.

By this point, Dot was convinced John Anderson, if that was his real name, had something to hide. But it had taken her just short of an hour to get this far, and she still had a day's worth of background checks to do.

She didn't think Steve would be happy about that.

Dot updated the file note with her findings, and her recommendation to proceed with personal criminal and credit checks for the candidate, and registration histories for the businesses.

She popped the files in her drawer, locked it, and went for a brisk walk around the floor. On the second lap, she stopped at the bathroom and the kitchen for instant coffee, then went back to her desk to do the reference checks.

The rest of the day passed without anything suspicious presenting itself, and it was time to check in with Steve, almost before she knew it. She almost danced to the door and tapped on the door with a smart rhythm.

"How are you getting along Dot? No problems or queries?"

"No, it's going well. I'm on target with the background checks."

"And what about the Anderson file?"

She grinned, "I think what I've discovered pretty much rules John Anderson out of proceeding to the next level of interviews."

"Okay, what are your grounds?"

"I've done some cursory checks of the websites of the businesses that employed him, and the information on-site doesn't tally up with the street view. One of the numbers on the second site is different to that on the reference and connects to something that sounds like a confused old man.

"If one of the websites was faulty that would be one thing, but all of them? It's just too coincidental."

"Go on."

"Our client is dealing with classified secrets, and the potential of a fraudulent application is too great a risk for the company to permit this early in the process."

"And if this applicant was a preferred candidate who was invited to apply?"

Dot thought considered the options.

"Then it would be necessary to look a little deeper to uncover evidence of fraud."

"And how would you do that?"

She listed them off on her fingers, "One, have an internal investigator verify the 100 points check in person to validate that the documents do exist and at least appear genuine. Then order copies from the original sources to validate them from central records.

"Two, order Federal Police and credit reference file checks.

"Three, order detailed business checks to verify the company details."

"Good work," Steve said with a small congratulatory smile, "I'll hold onto this and order the checks you recommend. Then I'll transfer the file to investigations, and mark it for return to you.

"Our investigators usually sight the original identification documents when they take the fingerprints anyway, and the file is updated with their in-person impressions at the time.

"Anderson will probably fall over himself to get this done, and it will seem to him that everything is proceeding well.

"And a good call with this one. Imagine if you had let it go when I first challenged you on this."

Dot smiled and bowed her head a little at the praise.

"If there's nothing else?"

She shook her head, and he indicated the files. She picked them up and walked to the door.

"Wait." She shifted the files to rest on her hip and frowned as she thought through the implications of a "preferred" candidate.

"If Anderson was recommended by someone inside the company, we should look into that person as well."

Steve tilted his head quizzically.

"Well, perhaps Anderson has some kind of leverage over that person. Like a gambling debt, or drug habit, or compromising photographs."

Steve narrowed his eyes at her, and then pointed at the chair, "elaborate."

"If you needed access to the company to retrieve some kind of information, one of the easiest ways would be to blackmail them."

"Wouldn't you just approach a senior officer and get to know them?"

"Well, that's one way, but look at us here at Wilkinson's. Our fields of interest and responsibility are quite narrow, taking out a Senior Executive wouldn't do any good if it wasn't the right one…

"Wait a minute, how did the vacancy come about?"

Steve typed something on his computer, paused, and said, "ski accident."

They looked at each other for a moment as the stakes raised around them.

"Well, that puts a slightly different complexion on things doesn't it?" he asked.

Dot scrubbed her face with both hands, "it's like some kind of spy movie. I feel like John

Anderson isn't going to be this guy's real name, don't you?"

"I'm sorry. At this point, I'm going to have to take this file from you and hand it on to someone more appropriate than a new employee on her second day at work."

"But—"

Steve stood up, "in the usual scheme of things you would have performed the reference checks and that's all. You don't have the knowledge or experience to carry this out any further."

Dot stood, "but—"

"I'm sorry. I'll keep you informed."

She had no option but to nod and leave the office. Her feet dragging, she deposited the files back to the records office, cleared her desk and left the building with a heavy heart.

With a night to stew it over, the next day she went into work, resolute in her intention to see what else she could dig up.

Another latte, and another hedgehog from the café, another impatient dance in the queue for her files for the day.

And then she was ready for what she hoped would be a covert search for John Anderson.

Nothing overly suspicious in the search engines, though without access to a photo she couldn't really tell. The social media accounts seemed relatively recent, with few posts, but again that wasn't unusual. Some people took to them, and others didn't.

Inspired by Nancy Drew and Trixie Belden, her intention to become a private investigator had ruled out many things people her age adopted. Like social media, and who's to say John Anderson wasn't the same.

And then the internet cut out.

In fact, it wasn't just the internet, it was her whole computer.

As if someone had just thrown a switch and shut it down.

She lifted her head to look up and around the office, and no one else seemed to be alert or alarmed by a shutdown.

And as she looked around, she noticed the cameras for the first time.

The closest one had a little red light that was blinking at her.

So, her activities had not been as covert as she's thought.

She nodded at the camera, put her headset on, and started making the day's calls.

That afternoon, when she met Steve for her usual daily review, she was filled with dread.

She curled inwards over the files clutched to her chest as she entered his office, expecting him to sack her.

"No problems?" he asked.

THE FIRST RUNG

She swallowed and shook her head mutely.

"I know you've been looking up John Anderson. I understand you think you're some kind of Nancy Drew, but you must learn when you can go it alone, and when you need to call on specialist advice."

Feeling suddenly 12 years old again, she nodded mutely and refused to meet his eyes while she tried to remember what she'd written on her job application.

"For god's sake, even Nancy Drew got help now and again from Bess, George, and Ned!"

Surprised, she looked up at him.

"Daughters," he said and rolled his eyes.

Dot laughed.

"Okay, okay, I get it."

"We're good now?"

She nodded, and stood, collecting the files up.

"Dot?" he waited until she met his eyes, "you know you can ask me anything?"

He held her gaze for a long time, long enough to make the point.

So.

She could ask him anything, as long as it was the right question.

She nodded and turned away.

What was the right question for a girl on the third day of her new job?

17

With a night to think it over, she thought she might have the right question. Though it was probably quite impertinent for her fourth day at work.

She made her calls, and when the time came to report to Steve, her heart was pounding in her chest, and her mouth was dry.

Once the daily checks were out of the way, she asked her question, "Might I be permitted to attend the briefing meetings about the Anderson file?"

Steve looked at her steadily, reading her.

"A new investigations team has been formed to deal with Anderson, and I'm prepared to let you join it as admin support—"

She let out a noise that was half squeal and half sigh as she relaxed into the chair.

He smiled tolerantly, "but you must remember you don't own this investigation. You're just there to provide admin support."

"Thank you," she said, "I won't let you down."

"You'll still be on probation, so if you mess up, you'll be out the door."

He stood up and walked around the desk.

Dot stood up as he held out his hand, putting hers into his.

"This is probably goodbye. You'll be ready for a new challenge when the team finishes its investigation, and if you do well, the

THE FIRST RUNG

Investigations Division will put you where they need you."

"Thank you. I'm a little scared now that I'm..."

"Nonsense. You've got a good brain in your head, and if you keep doing what you do, you'll go far."

She wiped a tear from the corner of her eye. "Right. Well, I'll just drop this lot off and go."

"Yes. Clear your desk tonight, and start on Level 15 tomorrow."

Dot told herself not to get too excited. She was just starting to get comfortable in her job, and now she had another, with no idea what to expect.

But if there really was a career ladder, it seemed like she might have climbed the first rung already.

THE END

ABOUT THE AUTHOR

Alexandria Blaelock writes stories, some of them for *Ellery Queen's Mystery Magazine* and *Pulphouse Fiction Magazine*. She's also written five self-help books applying business techniques to personal matters like getting dressed, cleaning house, and feeding your friends.

She lives in a forest because she enjoys birdsong, the scent of gum leaves and the sun on her face. When not telecommuting to parallel universes from her Melbourne based imagination, she watches K-dramas, talks to animals, and drinks Campari. At the same time.

Discover more at www.alexandriablaelock.com.

Lightning Source UK Ltd.
Milton Keynes UK
UKHW041955031122
411527UK00011B/144